Pokémon

FAVORITE FIRST FRIENDS!

BY C. J. NESTOR

A Random House PICTUREBACK® Book

Random House 🏠 New York

© 2018 The Pokémon Company International. © 1995–2018 Nintendo / Creatures Inc. / GAME FREAK inc. TM, ®, and character names are trademarks of Nintendo.
Published in the United States by Random House Children's Books, a division of Penguin Random House LLC, 1745 Broadway, New York, NY 10019, and in Canada by Penguin Random House Canada Limited, Toronto. Pictureback, Random House, and the Random House colophon are registered trademarks of Penguin Random House LLC.
ISBN 978-1-5247-7290-1
rhcbooks.com
Printed in the United States of America
10 9 8 7 6 5 4 3 2 1

ALOLA!

My name's **PROFESSOR KUKUI**, and I'm the Pokémon professor here on **ALOLA**! Alola is an island paradise, with warm, sandy beaches and beautiful mountains. It's also chock-full of Pokémon!

Trainers enjoy the sun, explore the land, and collect and battle all the Pokémon we have in Alola!

Each region in the Pokémon world has its own three first partner Pokémon that are Grass-type, Fire-type, and Water-type Pokémon. Nearly all young Trainers choose one of these Pokémon to accompany them on their first adventures!

Trainers who start their adventures in the **KANTO** region can choose between the Grass-type **BULBASAUR**, the Fire-type **CHARMANDER**, or the Water-type **SQUIRTLE** as their first partner Pokémon!

BULBASAUR stores a seed in the large bulb on its back. As it gathers sunlight, the seed on its back grows. I wonder what happens when the seed gets really large.

BULBASAUR
Category: Seed Pokémon
Height: 2'04" / **Weight:** 15.2 lbs.
Type: Grass-Poison

Watch out for the flame on **CHARMANDER**'s tail! When this Pokémon gets fired up, its tail burns bright and hot. I bet that comes in handy during Pokémon battles!

CHARMANDER
Category: Lizard Pokémon
Height: 2'00" / **Weight:** 18.7 lbs.
Type: Fire

Check out the shell on **SQUIRTLE**! Its smooth surface lets Squirtle swim at high speeds, and protects it from attacks. That strong defense makes it really tough in battle.

SQUIRTLE
Category: Tiny Turtle Pokémon
Height: 1'08" / **Weight:** 19.8 lbs.
Type: Water

Have you heard of **JOHTO?** Trainers who start their journey here pick between the Grass-type **CHIKORITA**, the Fire-type **CYNDAQUIL**, or the Water-type **TOTODILE!**

CHIKORITA

Category: Leaf Pokémon
Height: 2'11" / **Weight:** 14.1 lbs.
Type: Grass

CHIKORITA is a very friendly Pokémon. The leaf on its head smells sweet and makes everyone feel calm and happy. But when in battle, watch out, because this Pokémon can be as fierce as it is friendly!

CYNDAQUIL
Category: Fire Mouse Pokémon
Height: 1'08" / Weight: 17.4 lbs.
Type: Fire

When **CYNDAQUIL** is ready to fight, the fire on its back flares up, protecting it. But when it's sleepy, Cyndaquil's flames are small and sputter fitfully.

TOTODILE
Category: Big Jaw Pokémon
Height: 2'00" / **Weight:** 20.9 lbs.
Type: Water

Trainers who choose **TOTODILE** as their partner are in for a good time! This playful little Pokémon will show affection, but watch out for its bite. Its jaws are very powerful, and sometimes it doesn't know its own strength!

Trainers from the **HOENN** region won't see any of those previously discovered first partner Pokémon. Instead, they get their choice of the Grass-type **TREECKO**, the Fire-type **TORCHIC**, or the Water-type **MUDKIP**!

TREECKO has a thick tail, but what you really have to watch out for are its feet. It uses tiny hooks on its feet to climb trees and can attack from above. Look out below!

TREECKO
Category: Wood Gecko Pokémon
Height: 1'08" / **Weight:** 11.0 lbs.
Type: Grass

TORCHIC seems like a perfect cuddle buddy with its soft feathers and inner fire. But this little Pokémon can produce flames so hot, they will leave its foes scorched black.

TORCHIC
Category: Chick Pokémon
Height: 1'04" / **Weight:** 5.5 lbs.
Type: Fire

MUDKIP

Category: Mud Fish Pokémon
Height: 1'04" / **Weight:** 16.8 lbs.
Type: Water

MUDKIP is really cute with all those fins, but they don't just look good. They also let Mudkip sense movement in the water and air around it, so it knows what's happening without opening its eyes.

Trainers who start their adventures in the **SINNOH** region normally choose between the Grass-type **TURTWIG**, the Fire-type **CHIMCHAR**, or the Water-type **PIPLUP**.

TURTWIG has a shell, but it's nothing like Squirtle's. This Pokémon's shell is made of hard-packed soil. Turtwig's whole body absorbs sunlight and water for energy.

TURTWIG
Category: Tiny Leaf Pokémon
Height: 1'04" / **Weight:** 22.5 lbs.
Type: Grass

CHIMCHAR

Category: Chimp Pokémon
Height: 1'08" / **Weight:** 13.7 lbs.
Type: Fire

CHIMCHAR has a flame on its back that flickers if it isn't feeling well. However, Chimchar's flame never goes out, even in the rain. Amazing!

PIPLUP are often stubborn and won't listen to their Trainers. However, if you work really hard, you'll be friends for life with the Penguin Pokémon!

PIPLUP
Category: Penguin Pokémon
Height: 1'04" / **Weight:** 11.5 lbs.
Type: Water

Trainers who start their adventures in the **UNOVA** region are likely to choose between the Grass-type **SNIVY**, the Fire-type **TEPIG**, or the Water-type **OSHAWOTT**.

SNIVY loves the sun. Basking in sunlight makes its movements swifter. It uses vines better than you use your hands, so keep an eye out for it where you least expect!

TEPIG
Category: Fire Pig Pokémon
Height: 1'08" / **Weight:** 21.8 lbs.
Type: Fire

SNIVY
Category: Grass Snake Pokémon
Height: 2'00" / **Weight:** 17.9 lbs.
Type: Grass

Trainers who want **TEPIG** as their first companion should like well-done food! This little Pokémon shoots fireballs out of its nose to roast berries to eat.

OSHAWOTT is a small, fierce Pokémon. The scalchop on its stomach isn't just for breaking open hard berries; this shell is also a sharp weapon for use in battle!

OSHAWOTT
Category: Sea Otter Pokémon
Height: 1'08" / **Weight:** 13.0 lbs.
Type: Water

The first partner Pokémon unique to the **KALOS** region are the Grass-type **CHESPIN**, the Fire-type **FENNEKIN**, and the Water-type **FROAKIE!**

Trainers need to be careful if **CHESPIN** is their first partner Pokémon. The quills on its head are soft, but when it's getting ready for battle, they become sharp enough to pierce rock! Trainers should make sure their Chespin is relaxed and happy before they try patting its head.

CHESPIN
Category: Spiny Nut Pokémon
Height: 1'04" / **Weight:** 19.8 lbs.
Type: Grass

Watch out for the powerful Fire-type **FENNEKIN**! This Pokémon's cute ears are actually a vent for the superheated air inside its body. Youch!

FENNEKIN
Category: Fox Pokémon
Height: 1'04" / **Weight:** 20.7 lbs.
Type: Fire

FROAKIE's bubbles protect its sensitive skin from damage. This makes Froakie tough to beat!

FROAKIE
Category: Bubble Frog Pokémon
Height: 1'00" / **Weight:** 15.4 lbs.
Type: Water

Of course, some Trainers start their adventures right here in Alola! Trainers beginning in Alola get their choice of the Grass-type **ROWLET**, the Fire-type **LITTEN**, or the Water-type **POPPLIO**!

ROWLET

Category: Grass Quill Pokémon
Height: 1'00" / **Weight:** 3.3 lbs.
Type: Grass-Flying

ROWLET spends most of its day soaking up sunlight. It uses the energy it stores during the day to be more active at night. In battle, Rowlet will fly up to its foes and unleash a flurry of kicking attacks, so watch out!

POPPLIO is a hardworking Pokémon, and it's always fun to have around. It blows bubbles out its nose and puts in lots of practice so it can use these as a weapon in battle!

POPPLIO
Category: Sea Lion Pokémon
Height: 1'04" / **Weight:** 16.5 lbs.
Type: Water

When **LITTEN** grooms itself, it stores extra fur inside its stomach. When it wants to attack, it coughs up the fur and sets it on fire, igniting its burning attacks!

LITTEN
Category: Fire Cat Pokémon
Height: 1'04" / **Weight:** 9.5 lbs.
Type: Fire

Each of these first partner Pokémon can grow stronger and evolve into more-powerful Pokémon, like these evolutions of the Alola partners!

TORRACAT
Type: Fire

BRIONNE
Type: Water

DARTRIX
Type: Grass-Flying

Each Pokémon has its own strengths, weaknesses, and abilities. To learn more about them, you know what to do!

DECIDUEYE
Type: Grass-Ghost

Gotta catch 'em all!

PRIMARINA
Type: Water-Fairy

INCINEROAR
Type: Fire-Dark